TABLE OF CONTENT

Chapter 1: Trust and Treachery

Nature of trust in a survival situation 1

Consequences of broken trust 2

Identifying and assessing trustworthy individuals 4

Chapter 2: Survival Instincts 7

Fight-or-flight response and its impact on behavior 7

Physiological adaptations to extreme conditions 8

Strategies for sustaining physical and mental well-being 10

Chapter 3: The Bonds of Humanity 13

Importance of human connection in times of crisis 13

Challenges and opportunities for forming alliances 14

Role of empathy and compassion in survival 16

Chapter 4: The Shadows of Doubt 19

Psychological toll of prolonged uncertainty and fear 19

Dangers of paranoia and distrust 20

Maintaining mental resilience amidst adversity 22

Chapter 5: The Value of Knowledge 25

Importance of practical skills and experience in survival 25

Role of learning and adapting in a constantly changing environment 26

Balancing risk and reward in decision-making 28

Chapter 6: The Price of Leadership 31

Challenges and responsibilities of assuming leadership 31

Importance of trust and communication within the group..........32

Ethical dilemmas and sacrifices faced by leaders 34

Chapter 7: Redemption and Forgiveness 36

Potential for redemption in a world marked by betrayal 36

Power of forgiveness to heal wounds and strengthen bonds........37

Role of morality and compassion in a survival narrative 39

Chapter 8: The Weight of Secrets 41

Impact of secrets on trust and group dynamics.........................41

Challenges of keeping secrets in a small and isolated community 42

Moral implications of keeping or revealing secrets....................44

Chapter 9: The Triumph of Hope 47

Importance of maintaining hope in the face of adversity 47

Sources of hope and inspiration in extreme circumstances 48

Role of hope in shaping the outcome of survival.......................50

Chapter 1: Trust and Treachery

Nature of trust in a survival situation

The first chapter, "Trust and Treachery," in "The Safekeep" throws readers into a world where the very foundation of human interaction, trust, is put to the ultimate test. Survival, in the face of a devastating global catastrophe, becomes a grim dance of self-preservation where the bonds of friendship, family, and community are constantly challenged by the primal instinct to survive. The protagonist, whose name remains a mystery for much of the early narrative, finds themselves thrust into a harsh new reality. The world they once knew is shattered, and their initial instinct is to navigate the chaos alone. However, the very nature of the crisis forces them to consider the potential of trust as a vital tool for survival. .

The book utilizes a stark contrast between the protagonist's initial distrust and their gradual understanding of the necessity of collaboration. The protagonist, initially hardened by the cruel realities of the new world, finds themselves increasingly drawn to the possibility of connection. They are haunted by the memories of loved ones lost and the desperate need to find meaning in a world seemingly devoid of it. The world has become a landscape of mistrust, where even the closest companions can become potential threats. Every encounter is fraught with the possibility of betrayal, every act of kindness met with suspicion. The characters are forced to grapple with the agonizingly complex question of who to trust, a question that becomes even more pressing as they encounter individuals whose motivations are shrouded in mystery. .

The protagonist's gradual shift towards trust is not a simple leap of faith, but a measured response to the dire circumstances they face. The world has become a place where isolation can be just as deadly as a direct attack. It is through acts of kindness, shared vulnerabilities, and a shared understanding of the fragility of life that the protagonist begins to chip away at the walls they have erected around themselves. The protagonist's journey is one of gradual understanding, a recognition that true survival, in this new world, may not be about individual strength alone, but the ability to forge bonds of trust with others. .

The narrative underscores the importance of empathy and compassion in a world where fear and suspicion reign supreme. Through their interactions with other survivors, the protagonist learns that even in the face of unimaginable hardship, the capacity for human connection remains. Trust, in this context, becomes not just a matter of faith, but a strategy for survival. It is through acts of generosity, shared burdens, and mutual vulnerability that the characters begin to rebuild a sense of community, a fragile hope in the face of overwhelming despair. .

The world of "The Safekeep" presents a chillingly realistic portrayal of the consequences of societal collapse. It is a world where the fragility of human connection is constantly challenged by the raw, desperate need for survival. The narrative forces readers to confront the question of how far they would go to protect themselves and the people they care about. The reader, alongside the protagonist, is forced to confront the complex ethical and moral dilemmas of trust in a world stripped of its former rules. The book ultimately leaves the reader pondering the enduring power of human connection and the potential for hope even in the darkest of times.

Consequences of broken trust

"The Safekeep" isn't just a story of survival, it's a chilling exploration of the fragility of trust, a vital resource in the face of unimaginable peril. The very fabric of human connection, woven with threads of faith and reliance, is tested and frayed, revealing the devastating consequences of broken trust. This breakdown, meticulously portrayed in Chapter 1, "Trust and Treachery," sets the stage for a narrative where survival hinges on an unwavering commitment to honesty and vulnerability.

The consequences of broken trust manifest in a multitude of ways, each echoing the pervasive sense of fear and uncertainty that permeates the narrative. Firstly, broken trust erodes the fundamental building blocks of cooperation, hindering collective action and survival. This is exemplified in the initial scene of the book, where a group of survivors, burdened by the weight of betrayal and distrust, are unable to coordinate their efforts against a common enemy. The lack of faith in each other leads to paranoia, suspicion, and ultimately, isolation.

This erosion of trust creates an atmosphere of constant vigilance, where every interaction is fraught with suspicion. Characters constantly grapple with the weight of their past betrayals, forcing them to second-guess every word and action. The story becomes a tense, claustrophobic journey, where the fear of being betrayed casts a long shadow over every aspect of their existence.

Furthermore, the consequences of broken trust extend far beyond individual relationships. The collective trust within the community, so vital for their survival, is irrevocably shattered, leading to a breakdown in social order. With every betrayal, the bonds of community weaken, replaced by a culture of fear and suspicion, leaving survivors vulnerable to internal conflicts and external threats.

In this shattered landscape, characters struggle to navigate a world devoid of reliable anchors. The consequences of broken trust are deeply personal, leading to feelings of isolation, loneliness, and a profound sense of loss. The survivors are trapped in a vicious cycle, where past betrayals continue to haunt their present and impede their ability to forge meaningful connections.

The consequences of broken trust are not solely confined to the emotional realm. They manifest in tangible consequences, hindering the group's ability to acquire resources, manage conflicts, and defend themselves. Trust is the essential lubricant for any functional community, and its absence creates a crippling paralysis. .

However, the story is not without hope. The book explores the complexities of forgiveness and the possibility of rebuilding trust, albeit a challenging and arduous journey. The characters' struggle to overcome past betrayals and establish new bonds of trust highlights the resilience of the human spirit, the desperate need for connection, and the enduring power of hope.

"The Safekeep" serves as a stark reminder of the devastating impact of broken trust, a resource as vital as food and water for human survival. The story emphasizes the importance of cultivating and preserving trust, not only as a foundation for individual well-being but as a cornerstone for collective resilience. The characters' journey, fraught with the consequences of broken trust, illuminates the urgent need to prioritize honesty, vulnerability, and unwavering commitment to fostering genuine connections in the face of adversity.

Identifying and assessing trustworthy individuals

In a world ravaged by a cataclysmic event, trust becomes a precious commodity. "The Safekeep" doesn't merely present this concept, it immerses us in its stark reality, forcing characters to navigate a landscape where survival hinges on the ability to discern genuine intentions from the allure of self-preservation. The book dissects the intricacies of establishing trust in a world where survival instincts often overshadow empathy, creating a compelling narrative tapestry woven with threads of suspicion, vulnerability, and desperate hope.

The central protagonist, whose identity remains shrouded in mystery for a significant portion of the narrative, becomes a focal point for exploring the challenges of identifying trustworthy individuals. Thrust into a world of survivors grappling with profound loss and the raw instinct to survive, the protagonist is forced to confront their own biases and preconceived notions about trust. Initially relying on a perceived hierarchy of 'worthiness' – a doctor, a soldier, a scientist – the protagonist encounters a harsh reality: the true measure of trustworthiness transcends professions and social constructs. .

Instead, the book presents a nuanced understanding of trust built on observation, intuition, and empathy. The protagonist learns to read subtle cues, to decipher the unspoken language of survival, and to discern genuine concern from a façade of helpfulness. Through a series of encounters, each presenting unique challenges, the protagonist learns to assess individuals based on their actions, their motivations, and their willingness to sacrifice their own comfort for the benefit of others.

The book doesn't shy away from the complexities of human nature, showcasing individuals who oscillate between self-serving motives and genuine altruism. Trust, therefore, isn't presented as a binary concept; it's a constantly evolving dynamic, tested and refined through each interaction. Characters like the hardened soldier, initially perceived as untrustworthy, demonstrate their capacity for compassion and loyalty, while seemingly harmless individuals reveal darker intentions. This constant shift in perceptions compels the protagonist to remain vigilant, to question assumptions, and to embrace the fluidity of trust in a world defined by uncertainty.

The book skillfully weaves individual journeys into the larger tapestry of survival. The protagonist's own vulnerabilities and fears are exposed, making their struggle for trust relatable and authentic. This vulnerability, in turn, becomes a catalyst for genuine connection. By acknowledging their own limitations and their need for support, the protagonist opens themselves to the possibility of true trust. This vulnerability, in turn, draws out the best in those around them, revealing the hidden pockets of compassion that lie beneath the surface of a world ravaged by fear.

"The Safekeep" ultimately posits that trust is a delicate dance, requiring constant negotiation and a willingness to confront one's own biases. It's not a matter of finding the "perfect" individual; it's about recognizing the inherent flaws and potential for both good and evil in everyone. The protagonist's journey serves as a poignant reminder that in a world stripped bare, trust is not simply a matter of survival, but a powerful testament to the enduring human capacity for connection and hope.

Chapter 2: Survival Instincts

Fight-or-flight response and its impact on behavior

The human response to threat, the fight-or-flight reaction, is a primal instinct that dictates our survival. In "The Safekeep," this instinct becomes a powerful narrative force, shaping characters' actions, relationships, and ultimately, their fate. The book, weaving a tale of trust, survival, and human connection amidst dire circumstances, uses the fight-or-flight response as a lens through which to explore the complex interplay of fear, instinct, and the human desire for connection. .

When faced with imminent danger, the fight-or-flight response triggers a cascade of physiological changes. Adrenaline surges, heart rate quickens, and the body prepares for immediate action. This primal response, while designed to protect, can also distort perception and judgment. In the narrative, individuals react to the threats posed by the encroaching darkness, the unknown, and the growing uncertainty, their actions often dictated by the urgency of their survival instincts. .

The fight-or-flight response, however, is not simply a mechanism for individual survival. It also has a profound impact on the dynamics of trust and betrayal within the group. The pressure to survive pushes individuals to prioritize their own safety, sometimes at the expense of their fellow survivors. This is highlighted in the book through moments of conflict, where the fight-or-flight response fuels suspicion, animosity, and even violence. The narrative explores the inherent tension between the need for individual survival and the desire to maintain trust and cooperation within the group.

The book, however, does not present a bleak portrayal of humanity driven solely by self-preservation. Instead, it reveals the fight-or-flight response as a catalyst for both betrayal and unexpected acts of compassion. While fear and survival instincts drive some characters to act selfishly, others find strength in the shared experience of danger. In moments of crisis, the need to survive becomes a shared burden, forging a bond of trust and solidarity. These acts of kindness, courage, and selflessness arise not in defiance of the fight-or-flight response, but in a conscious choice to transcend its limitations. .

"The Safekeep" ultimately explores the nuances of the fight-or-flight response, recognizing its power as a motivator for both destructive and redemptive behaviors. The narrative highlights how, in the face of extreme circumstances, the human capacity for both self-preservation and compassion can emerge as opposing forces, dictating individual choices and shaping the collective fate of the group. The fight-or-flight response becomes a powerful narrative device, amplifying the tension between survival instincts and the enduring human desire for connection.

Physiological adaptations to extreme conditions

The human body, a marvel of intricate systems and resilient capabilities, possesses an uncanny ability to adapt to the most extreme of environments. This adaptability, driven by physiological mechanisms honed over millennia, is the cornerstone of survival in situations where the line between life and death is razor-thin. Chapter 2 of "The Safekeep" delves into these remarkable adaptations, revealing the silent battles fought within our very being as we confront the unforgiving forces of nature. .

When confronted with the chilling embrace of sub-zero temperatures, the body activates a cascade of physiological responses designed to conserve precious heat. Vasoconstriction, a narrowing of blood vessels, diverts blood flow away from the extremities, prioritizing core temperature maintenance. Shivering, a seemingly involuntary tremor, utilizes muscle contractions to generate heat, akin to an internal furnace. And the body's very metabolism, the complex web of chemical reactions that power life, slows down, conserving energy while minimizing heat loss. These adaptations are not merely passive responses; they are intricate maneuvers, orchestrated by the body's internal command center, to ensure survival in the face of a relentless cold.

Just as the body confronts the icy grip of winter, it also adapts to the searing heat of scorching deserts. Sweating, a simple act, becomes a lifeline, allowing for evaporative cooling as the body's natural cooling mechanism. The body's internal thermostat, sensing the rising temperature, triggers a cascade of physiological responses. Blood vessels dilate, bringing blood closer to the surface of the skin, facilitating heat dissipation. The body's rate of respiration increases, promoting the release of excess heat through exhaled air. And the body's electrolyte balance is meticulously regulated to prevent dehydration, a silent killer in extreme heat. These adaptations, finely tuned by evolution, are the body's shield against the unrelenting assault of high temperatures.

At the heart of these adaptations lies a remarkable concept: homeostasis. This delicate balance, the body's tireless struggle to maintain a stable internal environment, is the bedrock of survival. When faced with extreme conditions, the body does not simply succumb; it actively fights back, leveraging its internal arsenal to maintain this delicate equilibrium. The body's ability to regulate temperature, fluid balance, and energy expenditure, while seemingly mundane, are testaments to the intricate workings of life itself. These adaptations are not mere biological curiosities; they are the silent heroes, working tirelessly behind the scenes, ensuring our survival in the face of unrelenting adversity.

"The Safekeep" weaves these physiological adaptations into the narrative tapestry, illustrating their critical role in the survival of its characters. The protagonists, thrust into dire circumstances, rely on their bodies' innate resilience to endure the hardships they face. The book's narrative, enriched by these scientific insights, underscores the profound connection between human resilience and the body's innate capacity to adapt. .

The book delves beyond the immediate physiological responses, highlighting the long-term impact of extreme conditions on the human body. Chronic exposure to cold, for example, can lead to a thickening of subcutaneous fat, an insulating layer against the relentless chill. Similarly, prolonged exposure to high altitude can induce physiological changes in the body's red blood cell count, boosting oxygen-carrying capacity in thin air. These adaptations, while gradual and often invisible, are testaments to the body's capacity for adaptation, its ability to sculpt itself to the demands of its environment.

"The Safekeep" underscores the intricate relationship between the human body and its environment, highlighting the extraordinary resilience of our species. The book offers a glimpse into the silent struggles of survival, showcasing the physiological adaptations that allow us to endure even the most extreme of conditions. In doing so, it emphasizes the remarkable capacity of the human body, a testament to the power of evolution and the very essence of life itself.

Strategies for sustaining physical and mental well-being

The Safekeep dives deep into the human psyche, exploring the raw and visceral reactions to life-altering situations. The narrative unfurls, weaving together themes of trust, survival, and the human connection in the face of imminent danger. Within the confines of this perilous journey, the characters navigate the complexities of their own inner landscapes, desperately seeking strategies to preserve their physical and mental well-being. .

The text demonstrates how survival transcends mere physical endurance. It demands a delicate dance between maintaining physical strength and nurturing mental resilience. Characters grapple with the harsh realities of their predicament, finding solace in small acts of kindness and moments of shared vulnerability. The narrative underscores that in such dire circumstances, the human need for connection and empathy becomes a fundamental survival instinct.

The Safekeep meticulously showcases how the characters employ various coping mechanisms to stay afloat. They tap into their inherent resilience, utilizing their resourcefulness to navigate the unknown. The book portrays a diverse range of coping mechanisms, from practical skills of resource management and shelter construction to the profound power of storytelling and shared memories. These acts become a lifeline, anchoring them to a sense of purpose and shared humanity. .

The narrative highlights the importance of maintaining a sense of normalcy, even in the midst of chaos. Routines become an anchor, providing structure and a sense of control in a situation where everything feels unpredictable. The characters demonstrate a remarkable capacity to adapt, drawing upon their past experiences and knowledge to shape their present reality. .

Mental well-being, the book posits, is not merely a luxury but a necessity for survival. The characters recognize the importance of fostering hope, even when faced with seemingly insurmountable odds. Humor, a powerful tool for emotional regulation, emerges as a vital coping mechanism. The narrative portrays how laughter can provide a much-needed respite from the relentless grip of fear and anxiety. .

The Safekeep underscores the value of self-reflection and introspection. Characters grapple with their own vulnerabilities, acknowledging their limitations while embracing their strengths. They learn to communicate their needs effectively, fostering an atmosphere of mutual support and understanding. This crucial act of self-awareness becomes a foundation for building trust, both within themselves and with those around them. .

The narrative emphasizes the profound impact of social connection and shared experiences on the individual's mental well-being. Characters find solace in acts of compassion and support, reminding us that even in the darkest of times, human connection can illuminate the path forward. Through shared stories, rituals, and traditions, they cultivate a sense of community, reminding us that our collective resilience is stronger than any individual hardship. .

The Safekeep offers a poignant exploration of the human capacity for resilience, demonstrating how even in the most dire circumstances, the will to survive can be fueled by our innate need for connection, hope, and a shared sense of purpose. The book emphasizes the importance of maintaining physical and mental well-being through a multifaceted approach that encompasses resourcefulness, emotional regulation, and the enduring power of human connection. The narrative serves as a poignant reminder that survival is not merely a physical endeavor, but a testament to the resilience of the human spirit.

Chapter 3: The Bonds of Humanity

Importance of human connection in times of crisis

The crucible of crisis exposes the raw essence of humanity, stripping away the veneer of societal constructs and revealing the primal need for connection. In the heart of this tumultuous process lies a profound truth: human connection is not simply a luxury, but a vital lifeline in the face of adversity. The very act of survival, in its most basic form, hinges on a shared vulnerability, a willingness to trust, and a profound understanding that individual strength is ultimately amplified by the collective. .

This inherent truth, amplified by the stark realities of a world ravaged by an unnamed catastrophe, forms the thematic core of _The Safekeep_. The narrative underscores the paramount importance of human connection in times of crisis, unveiling a tapestry of resilience interwoven with the threads of trust, compassion, and empathy. As characters grapple with the immediate threat of survival, their actions reveal a fundamental truth: isolation breeds fear and despair, while connection fosters hope and resilience.

The Safekeep presents a microcosm of humanity, stripped bare by the brutal realities of a world in flux. In the absence of pre-existing societal structures, the characters' interactions paint a vivid picture of how human connection becomes the very foundation of order, offering a sense of purpose and meaning amidst chaos. The narrative delves into the nuances of trust, demonstrating that it is not simply a binary choice, but a fragile construct built upon shared experiences, mutual understanding, and the willingness to be vulnerable. It is through these acts of vulnerability that characters forge profound connections, transcending individual survival to embrace a collective sense of purpose.

The characters' journeys, interwoven with moments of profound loss and heartbreak, reveal the transformative power of connection. In the face of immense hardship, it is the shared burden of grief, the whispers of comfort, and the simple act of listening that become the most powerful tools for healing. The narrative illustrates how human connection transcends the boundaries of language and culture, becoming a universal language of shared humanity. It is through this shared language that characters navigate the labyrinth of fear and uncertainty, offering solace to one another and reaffirming the intrinsic value of human connection in the face of insurmountable odds. .

The Safekeep does not shy away from the complexities of human nature. It delves into the spectrum of emotions that arise in the midst of crisis, showcasing the vulnerabilities, fears, and anxieties that can often lead to conflict and division. The narrative, however, does not succumb to despair. Instead, it underscores the enduring power of empathy and compassion, revealing the transformative capacity of human connection to bridge even the deepest of divides. Through acts of kindness, gestures of support, and the shared pursuit of a common goal, characters demonstrate the potential for unity even in the face of adversity. .

In a world stripped bare by crisis, _The Safekeep_ serves as a poignant testament to the enduring strength of human connection. The narrative, imbued with a sense of realism and hope, emphasizes the importance of trust, empathy, and compassion as the cornerstones of resilience. By showcasing the profound impact of human connection in shaping individual and collective destinies, the book provides a compelling reflection on the very essence of what it means to be human.

Challenges and opportunities for forming alliances

The novel "The Safekeep" paints a vivid picture of human resilience and the complex dynamics of trust in the face of overwhelming adversity. The narrative throws its characters into a world stripped bare, where the familiar comforts of civilization have been replaced by the harsh realities of survival. This crucible of hardship forces individuals to confront their own vulnerabilities and the choices they must make in order to secure their existence. It is in this brutal environment that the formation of alliances becomes a pivotal factor in determining both survival and the preservation of humanity's core values.

The inherent challenges to forging alliances in this post-apocalyptic setting are multi-faceted. The most immediate challenge is the scarcity of resources. With food, shelter, and even clean water becoming precious commodities, competition for these essentials becomes fierce. Every interaction is fraught with potential danger, as trust is a luxury few can afford. Suspicion and distrust fester, fueled by the fear of betrayal, leaving individuals wary of extending their trust. The threat of violence, both from the remnants of a shattered society and the dangers of the ravaged landscape, further complicates the equation. The constant need for vigilance and self-preservation creates an environment where cooperation feels like a risky gamble.

However, amidst this atmosphere of suspicion and fear, the potential for genuine connection emerges. The novel highlights the innate human desire for companionship and the recognition that collaboration can be a crucial survival strategy. The characters grapple with the challenge of discerning genuine intentions from opportunism. The need to build trust becomes a constant struggle, demanding a careful assessment of potential allies. Characters find themselves navigating a delicate balance between maintaining their independence and acknowledging the benefits of collaboration. The inherent risks of vulnerability are weighed against the potential rewards of shared resources, knowledge, and protection.

The opportunity for alliances presents itself in the form of shared goals, common vulnerabilities, and the recognition of individual strengths and weaknesses. The characters begin to understand that their survival hinges on their ability to overcome their individual limitations and recognize the value of collective action. This recognition creates fertile ground for the blossoming of trust, as individuals realize that their collective strength far outweighs the potential risks of vulnerability.

The novel emphasizes the importance of shared values and a common understanding of what constitutes a just and humane world in forging enduring alliances. In a world where the old rules have been shattered, the characters are forced to grapple with the moral implications of their actions and the responsibility they bear to each other. The willingness to prioritize the collective good over individual gain becomes a crucial factor in building sustainable alliances. The bonds of humanity, forged through shared experiences and a commitment to shared values, become the cornerstone of trust and collaboration.

The novel presents a nuanced perspective on the challenges and opportunities of forming alliances in a world where the very essence of humanity is tested. The characters' journeys highlight the delicate balance between survival and the preservation of human dignity, demonstrating that even in the darkest of times, the bonds of trust and collaboration can hold the key to navigating the treacherous path towards a better future.

Role of empathy and compassion in survival

The heart of "The Safekeep" beats with the rhythm of survival, a pulse fueled by the flickering flame of human connection amidst a world teetering on the brink of oblivion. The narrative, woven through the tapestry of trust and vulnerability, unfurls the story of a society shattered by an unseen, cataclysmic event, where empathy and compassion become not mere virtues but vital tools for endurance. Chapter 3, "The Bonds of Humanity," serves as a crucial turning point, where the raw necessity of human connection is laid bare.

In the aftermath of the catastrophe, a sense of pervasive fear and distrust permeates the remnants of society. The world, once a familiar tapestry of interaction and shared experience, has become a perilous maze of suspicion. This palpable fear of the unknown and the fear of those who might exploit it, serves as a powerful force, tearing at the fabric of human connection. Yet, amidst this bleak panorama, a flicker of hope emerges. The protagonist, a young woman named Elara, finds herself thrust into a community of survivors struggling to piece together a semblance of existence. Elara, scarred by a past tainted by betrayal, harbors a deep distrust for others. The trauma of her past has hardened her heart, making her resistant to the fragile hope that others offer.

This is where the power of empathy and compassion comes into play. The community, despite their own anxieties and uncertainties, recognizes the depth of Elara's pain and reaches out with a tender, unspoken understanding. They offer solace without judgment, their acts of kindness whispering a silent promise of safety and belonging. This profound empathy, devoid of expectations, shatters Elara's fortress of distrust, slowly thawing her heart, brick by brick. .

In the crucible of their shared struggle, the survivors learn that compassion isn't a luxury, but a lifeline. It's in the sharing of meager rations, in the comfort offered during moments of despair, and in the willingness to extend a helping hand even when resources are scarce. The very act of caring for one another, even in the face of overwhelming adversity, becomes a potent countermeasure to the isolating despair that threatens to engulf them. .

However, the path of empathy and compassion is not without its challenges. The community's leader, a wise and seasoned woman named Anya, embodies the complexities of this virtue. Anya, a beacon of hope and resilience, faces the burden of leading a community where the scars of the past linger. She navigates this treacherous landscape with unwavering empathy, yet her compassion isn't a naive sentimentality, but a steely determination to safeguard the community's fragile unity. Anya's unwavering faith in the inherent goodness of humanity, even when faced with betrayals and anxieties, serves as a crucial reminder that in the face of unimaginable darkness, humanity's ability to connect and care for each other can be the single most potent weapon in the struggle for survival.

Chapter 3 goes beyond mere survival tactics, exploring the nuanced, often painful, journey of human connection. It reveals how empathy and compassion, even in the harshest of circumstances, can serve as a catalyst for forging enduring bonds, creating a sense of purpose and shared purpose that transcends the immediate fear of the unknown. The narrative underscores the fundamental truth that in the aftermath of devastation, empathy and compassion are not just emotional responses; they are the very building blocks upon which a new, albeit fragile, sense of hope can be erected. .

The chapter concludes with a poignant realization that the act of caring, of extending a hand to another in need, can be a profound and transformative act. The characters, stripped bare of their former identities, find solace in the knowledge that they are not alone. Their vulnerability, their shared grief, and their collective strength in the face of fear becomes a testament to the resilience of the human spirit, a spirit that finds solace in the bonds of human connection. .

This delicate balance between the harsh realities of survival and the transformative power of empathy and compassion forms the crux of "The Safekeep. " It is a narrative that resonates with the deepest human desires for connection and understanding, reminding us that even in the darkest of times, the shared flame of empathy can provide light and warmth, illuminating the path towards resilience and hope.

Chapter 4: The Shadows of Doubt

Psychological toll of prolonged uncertainty and fear

In the desolate landscape of "The Safekeep," a chilling tale unfolds, weaving a complex tapestry of trust, survival, and the profound psychological toll of prolonged uncertainty. The story's essence lies in the unwavering struggle of its characters, thrust into a desperate fight for existence against the relentless shadows of doubt and fear. The fourth chapter, titled "The Shadows of Doubt," delves into the very core of this psychological torment, revealing the insidious nature of prolonged uncertainty and its devastating impact on the human psyche.

Within this chapter, the narrative paints a vivid picture of the characters' descent into a state of profound unease and suspicion. The once familiar world, now shrouded in mystery and danger, becomes a breeding ground for fear and paranoia. Every whisper, every shadow, every unexpected sound becomes a source of potential threat. The constant fear of the unknown seeps into their very being, eroding their sense of security and leaving them perpetually on edge. .

The characters' ability to trust, a vital element for survival, is gradually chipped away by the relentless onslaught of uncertainty. The fragile threads of trust that once bound them together begin to fray, as each individual struggles to navigate the treacherous terrain of survival. The lingering fear of betrayal and the ever-present danger of manipulation become constant companions, further fueling the cycle of doubt and suspicion. .

The constant uncertainty breeds a pervasive sense of isolation, further exacerbating the psychological toll. Once-familiar faces become shrouded in a veil of suspicion, making it impossible to discern friend from foe. The characters find themselves trapped in a solitary existence, their minds consumed by the relentless fear of the unknown and the growing distrust of those around them. .

"The Safekeep" masterfully portrays the agonizing journey of the human spirit in the face of prolonged uncertainty. The characters grapple with the fear of the unknown, battling not only the physical threats that surround them but also the insidious psychological warfare waged within their own minds. The very act of survival becomes a constant battle against the ever-present shadows of doubt, fear, and suspicion. .

As the narrative progresses, the characters' internal struggles become increasingly apparent. Their actions, once driven by hope and trust, are now dictated by fear and suspicion. The erosion of their mental fortitude, a consequence of the prolonged uncertainty, becomes a stark reminder of the devastating impact of fear on the human psyche. .

The chapter's final scene leaves the reader with a sense of foreboding, highlighting the insidious nature of fear and its ability to undermine even the strongest bonds. The characters' future remains shrouded in uncertainty, leaving the reader to ponder the psychological toll of prolonged fear and the enduring power of doubt in the face of an uncertain future. .

The psychological toll of prolonged uncertainty and fear, as portrayed in "The Safekeep," is not merely a narrative device. It is a powerful exploration of the human psyche, exposing the fragility of trust, the relentless nature of fear, and the enduring struggle for survival in the face of the unknown. The story serves as a stark reminder of the psychological cost of prolonged uncertainty and the profound impact of fear on the human condition.

Dangers of paranoia and distrust

The gnawing tendrils of paranoia and distrust are a constant presence in "The Safekeep," a narrative that explores the fragile nature of human connection in the face of dire circumstances. The book, through its meticulously crafted characters and a gripping plot, illuminates the dangers of succumbing to suspicion, particularly in environments where survival hinges on collaboration.

Chapter 4, "The Shadows of Doubt," serves as a pivotal moment in the story, revealing the corrosive effects of paranoia and distrust. The narrative skillfully weaves a tapestry of fear, uncertainty, and suspicion, highlighting the insidious nature of these emotions. The chapter exposes how readily paranoia can take root, particularly when faced with the unknown, fostering an atmosphere of suspicion that poisons even the most robust bonds. The weight of survival hangs heavily, pushing characters to question their most cherished alliances, casting shadows of doubt over the very people they depend upon. .

As the story unfolds, the characters grapple with the insidious nature of distrust. They find themselves entangled in a web of speculation and accusations, their ability to discern truth from fiction blurred by the relentless grip of fear. The characters' actions, fueled by paranoia, often exacerbate the very situations they fear, leading to a vicious cycle of distrust and isolation. Their struggle to navigate this treacherous landscape underscores the immense destructive power of paranoia, revealing how readily it can undermine trust and shatter even the strongest bonds. .

"The Safekeep" deftly portrays how paranoia can distort perceptions, leading to misinterpretations and rash judgments. The characters' interpretations of events become warped by their anxieties, driving them to make decisions based on flimsy evidence and fueled by fear rather than reason. The chapter demonstrates how paranoia, unchecked, can turn individuals against one another, fostering an environment of suspicion and hostility. .

The chapter further emphasizes the dangers of paranoia by highlighting the insidious nature of distrust. Characters become hesitant to share information, fearing betrayal and manipulation.

This reluctance to communicate leads to a breakdown in communication, hampering their collective efforts to survive. The narrative underscores how distrust, born out of fear, can create a climate of isolation, hindering collaboration and ultimately jeopardizing their survival.

"The Safekeep," through the lens of Chapter 4, exposes the devastating consequences of succumbing to paranoia and distrust. The story illustrates how these negative emotions can corrupt judgment, erode trust, and ultimately lead to a spiral of self-destruction. The narrative underscores the vital importance of maintaining trust, even amidst adversity, as the foundation of a sustainable community and the key to overcoming the most challenging of circumstances.

Maintaining mental resilience amidst adversity

Chapter 4, "The Shadows of Doubt," of "The Safekeep" delves deeply into the psychological toll of enduring extreme hardship. This section unveils the human capacity to withstand immense adversity, illustrating how individuals can maintain their mental fortitude despite overwhelming challenges. The narrative, set against a backdrop of dire circumstances, explores the delicate interplay between trust, survival, and the human connection, revealing how these elements intertwine to shape the mental landscape of those navigating a crisis. .

The chapter's central character, a nameless protagonist, embodies the struggle to maintain mental resilience in the face of profound uncertainty. He has been thrust into a world where the familiar has been replaced by the unknown, where the past is a faded memory and the future an elusive promise. His journey through this world of shadows requires an almost superhuman ability to navigate the psychological labyrinth of doubt, fear, and despair. .

The protagonist's internal battle is not simply a personal struggle but a universal human experience. His journey mirrors the collective struggle of humanity to endure amidst chaos, to find meaning and purpose in the face of seemingly insurmountable odds. The author, through the protagonist's experiences, offers a profound exploration of the human psyche, revealing the intricate mechanisms that allow individuals to maintain their mental equilibrium even when the external world crumbles around them.

The Safekeep, a metaphorical representation of the protagonist's internal refuge, serves as a vital element in preserving his mental resilience. This inner sanctuary, a space of quiet reflection and unwavering hope, becomes his anchor in the storm of uncertainty. It is within this safekeep that he finds strength to confront the shadows of doubt, to challenge the internal narrative of fear, and to cultivate a sense of hope that sustains him through the darkest moments.

The protagonist's interactions with other characters, particularly those who share his predicament, illuminate the power of human connection in fostering mental resilience. Their shared vulnerability and the unspoken understanding that develops between them form a fragile but vital support system. The camaraderie forged in the crucible of adversity provides a vital lifeline, offering solace and validation in the face of profound isolation. .

The chapter highlights the importance of maintaining a sense of purpose in the face of adversity. The protagonist's unwavering commitment to survival, to the possibility of a better future, provides him with a compass, guiding him through the treacherous terrain of despair and uncertainty. This unwavering purpose, rooted in the innate human desire for meaning and belonging, becomes his guiding star, reminding him of the strength he possesses within.

"The Shadows of Doubt" offers a stark reminder of the fragility of the human psyche and the resilience that lies dormant within us. It underscores the importance of internal resources, the strength of human connection, and the transformative power of hope in navigating the complexities of human existence. Through the protagonist's harrowing journey, i paints a portrait of the human spirit, revealing its remarkable capacity to endure, to adapt, and to ultimately triumph over seemingly insurmountable challenges.

Chapter 5: The Value of Knowledge

Importance of practical skills and experience in survival

The stark reality of survival, often portrayed as a brutal struggle for existence, takes center stage in "The Safekeep. " This compelling narrative, steeped in the themes of trust, survival, and the enduring human connection, underscores the critical importance of practical skills and experience in navigating the direst of circumstances. .

The book's protagonist, facing a world ravaged by an unnamed catastrophe, finds themselves thrust into a reality where survival is a constant, arduous struggle. Food, water, and shelter become elusive necessities, and the absence of established societal structures necessitates a return to the fundamental basics of human existence. The protagonist's journey unveils the inherent fragility of human life and the critical role that practical skills play in navigating this volatile new world.

The narrative emphasizes the significance of knowledge that translates into tangible action, highlighting the stark difference between theoretical understanding and the practical application of survival skills. The protagonist's initial reliance on book knowledge, while a valuable starting point, proves insufficient in the face of real-world challenges. Their survival hinges on acquiring and refining practical skills such as foraging, hunting, building shelter, and navigating treacherous landscapes. These are no longer mere abstract concepts; they become the lifelines that separate survival from succumbing to the unforgiving elements.

"The Safekeep" goes beyond simply showcasing practical skills as a means of survival. It delves into the emotional and psychological impact of these skills, highlighting their ability to instil confidence and a sense of control in a chaotic world. The protagonist's newfound proficiency in practical skills, coupled with the challenges they overcome, fosters a sense of agency and resilience, allowing them to confront their fears and navigate the complexities of their new reality with renewed purpose. .

The narrative also explores the interconnectedness of practical skills and the human connection. The protagonist's journey emphasizes that survival is not merely a solitary endeavor; it is often a collaborative effort that relies on shared knowledge and skills. Their interactions with other survivors, both allies and antagonists, showcase the importance of understanding, respecting, and collaborating with others to enhance their collective chances of survival. .

The value of practical skills and experience is further amplified through the depiction of the protagonist's encounters with those who lack the necessary knowledge or aptitude. Their journey highlights the vulnerability of those who rely solely on theoretical knowledge or possess limited practical skills, highlighting the stark consequences of being unprepared for the harsh realities of survival.

Ultimately, "The Safekeep" powerfully underscores the crucial role of practical skills and experience in navigating a world where survival is not a guarantee but an ongoing, demanding struggle. It underscores the importance of embracing hands-on knowledge and the potential of human ingenuity and resilience in the face of adversity. By showcasing the protagonist's journey from vulnerability to self-reliance, the narrative implicitly champions the power of practical skills and experience as vital tools for navigating uncertain times and building a sustainable future.

Role of learning and adapting in a constantly changing environment

In the face of relentless change, the ability to learn and adapt becomes an existential imperative. "The Safekeep," a narrative built on the foundations of trust, survival, and the human connection in dire circumstances, vividly illustrates this point. The characters, thrust into an environment of constant flux and peril, are forced to confront the limitations of their pre-existing knowledge and embrace the necessity of continuous learning. The story unfolds as a testament to the human capacity for resilience, highlighting the power of knowledge acquisition and adaptability in overcoming adversity.

The protagonists, survivors of an unknown cataclysm, navigate a world where the familiar has crumbled and the rules of the old order are no longer applicable. The world they face is a canvas of uncertainty, where even the most fundamental aspects of survival require constant reevaluation. This compels them to shed their preconceived notions and engage in a relentless pursuit of knowledge, becoming students of their own survival. The book emphasizes the importance of not just absorbing information, but actively processing it, understanding its implications, and applying it strategically.

The characters' quest for knowledge extends beyond the practicalities of survival. They grapple with the emotional and psychological implications of their new reality, delving into the complexities of human nature in the face of immense pressure. This journey of self-discovery requires them to confront their own limitations, biases, and prejudices, shedding those aspects that impede their ability to adapt and build trust. They learn to recognize the value of diverse perspectives, acknowledging that each individual possesses a unique knowledge base that can contribute to the collective understanding of the world around them.

"The Safekeep" demonstrates that the learning process is not a linear progression but a series of iterative steps, punctuated by moments of failure and setbacks. These failures, far from being a cause for despair, become valuable lessons, shaping the characters' understanding of their environment and themselves. The protagonists learn to embrace the discomfort of the unknown, accepting that they may never have all the answers, and instead, focus on honing their skills in discerning credible information from the flood of misinformation.

Furthermore, the book highlights the importance of collaborative learning, emphasizing the collective intelligence that arises from the shared experience of a community facing a common challenge. Characters forge bonds of trust based on their willingness to share knowledge, skills, and resources. They recognize the value of collaboration, understanding that individual success is inextricably linked to the well-being of the collective. This collaborative approach, fueled by the constant exchange of knowledge, becomes a crucial element in their adaptation and survival.

The narrative culminates in a powerful demonstration of how learning and adaptation are not just a means to survive, but also a path to transcendence. The characters, through their journey of knowledge acquisition and emotional growth, emerge stronger, wiser, and more resilient. They discover that the true measure of survival is not just about physical endurance but about the capacity to adapt, evolve, and build a new world based on the lessons learned from the ashes of the old. In "The Safekeep," the characters are not merely surviving; they are learning, growing, and ultimately, transforming into a community of survivors, forging a new future built on the foundation of knowledge and trust.

Balancing risk and reward in decision-making

The precarious dance between risk and reward lies at the heart of survival, particularly in the desperate circumstances depicted in "The Safekeep. " Within the book's narrative, the characters are constantly faced with choices that demand a careful assessment of potential gains against potential losses. The need to secure resources, find safety, and navigate treacherous social landscapes compels them to weigh the odds, often with limited information and a heavy sense of uncertainty. .

The novel's protagonist, [Character name], exemplifies this constant balancing act. Their decision-making process is shaped by a deep understanding of their environment, an awareness of their own limitations, and a calculated willingness to take risks. For instance, when faced with the opportunity to acquire crucial supplies, they must consider the potential dangers posed by venturing into unknown territory. Their choice to take the risk is driven by a precise analysis of their needs, the available information, and their assessment of the likelihood of success. This meticulous approach highlights the critical nature of information in navigating risk. .

The concept of trust further complicates this calculus. The characters are forced to consider the potential rewards of collaboration, cooperation, and reliance on others, against the ever-present threat of betrayal. This tension is particularly evident in [Describe a specific scenario from the book where trust is a crucial element in decision-making]. The decision to [Action taken by characters] hinges on a calculated assessment of the trustworthiness of [Characters involved]. This dynamic highlights the inherent risk associated with vulnerability in a world where survival is paramount. .

The novel explores the psychological impact of these constant risk assessments. The characters are driven by a complex mix of fear, desperation, and hope. Their decisions are not always rational, often colored by emotional impulses and the weight of past experiences. [Provide a specific example from the book where emotional considerations influence decision-making and the associated risk]. The consequences of these choices, both positive and negative, serve as powerful lessons in the ongoing battle between instinct and calculated strategy. .

"The Safekeep" ultimately demonstrates that navigating risk and reward is a continuous, evolving process. It is not merely about making the right choices, but about adapting to changing circumstances, learning from mistakes, and constantly re-evaluating the landscape of potential gains and losses. This dynamic, interwoven with the themes of trust and human connection, drives the compelling narrative of survival and resilience that defines the book.

Chapter 6: The Price of Leadership

Challenges and responsibilities of assuming leadership

The sixth chapter of "The Safekeep" throws readers into the heart of leadership's complex dance, showcasing the myriad challenges and responsibilities that accompany the mantle of command. As the survivors, fractured and reeling from the sudden loss of their established authority, scramble to forge a new path, the narrative unflinchingly explores the difficult choices, the ethical dilemmas, and the personal sacrifices that define leadership in the face of unimaginable adversity.

The chapter meticulously unveils the weight of responsibility that falls upon those who step into the void, highlighting the impossible demands placed upon them. The decision to lead, in the face of fear, doubt, and the stark reality of limited resources, becomes a constant burden. Every choice carries the potential for life or death, for hope or despair, and those in leadership must navigate this perilous landscape with a clear head and a steady hand. .

"The Safekeep" doesn't shy away from the vulnerability of leadership. The characters, burdened with the knowledge that their decisions will shape the fate of their community, are forced to confront their own weaknesses and insecurities. The inherent fragility of leadership, even in the most capable of hands, is a constant reminder of the precariousness of their position.

The text delves into the intricate web of trust that forms the foundation of effective leadership. The survivors, stripped of their familiar structures and social norms, are forced to rely on instinct and the fragile threads of shared experience. The chapter explores the challenges of establishing and maintaining trust in an environment of uncertainty and fear, where individual agendas can easily clash with the greater good. The weight of leadership, in this context, is amplified by the responsibility to foster a sense of unity and shared purpose amongst the survivors.

Leadership, in "The Safekeep," is not a position of power or privilege, but rather a mantle of immense responsibility. It is the burden of making difficult choices, of offering hope in the face of despair, and of ultimately leading a community towards survival, even in the face of insurmountable odds. This chapter is not about glorifying leadership but rather about highlighting its profound human cost, the sacrifices it demands, and the unwavering strength it requires to sustain hope in the face of chaos.

Importance of trust and communication within the group

The importance of trust and communication within a group is not merely a theoretical concept in The Safekeep. It is a life-or-death necessity woven into the very fabric of the story, a testament to the human need for connection and collaboration in the face of overwhelming adversity. The narrative unfurls in a world devastated by an unknown cataclysm, where remnants of humanity struggle to survive in a hostile environment. The remnants of humanity are scattered, struggling to survive in a hostile environment. Within this bleak landscape, a group of individuals, bound by a shared history and a desperate need for survival, find solace in each other..

The story begins with a sense of isolation, a stark contrast to the interconnectedness that the world once knew. The characters, initially strangers to one another, are forced to come together. They forge a bond, not out of convenience or shared ideology, but out of a primal instinct to survive. Trust, initially fragile, is earned through shared hardship and demonstrated commitment. The ability to communicate effectively, to share burdens and vulnerabilities, is a constant battle against the ever-present fear and suspicion. Each member of the group carries a hidden past, a fear of betrayal, a personal baggage that threatens to unravel the fragile trust they've built.

The narrative emphasizes the complex dance between individual needs and the collective good. The characters must navigate their own desires and anxieties while recognizing the importance of collaboration. Their decisions, their actions, are driven by a constant negotiation between self-preservation and the survival of the group..

A crucial element of this negotiation is the communication of information. The characters are constantly battling misinformation, misinterpretations, and a deliberate withholding of facts. Each character's individual perspective, shaped by their unique experiences and vulnerabilities, colors their perception of reality. This inherent bias, if left unchecked, can lead to mistrust, fracturing the very foundation of their group dynamic..

The story delves into the intricate interplay of trust and communication, highlighting its essential role in shaping the group's trajectory. It underscores the transformative power of genuine communication, the ability to share fears, vulnerabilities, and aspirations. It demonstrates how the act of listening, of actively trying to understand another's perspective, can dismantle walls of suspicion and build bridges of trust..

As the characters navigate the complexities of survival, the reader is offered a powerful glimpse into the human spirit's resilience. The story highlights the innate desire for connection, the need to be understood, and the shared human longing for a semblance of normalcy in a world that has been irrevocably altered. It underscores the power of vulnerability, of letting down one's guard and allowing oneself to be seen..

Ultimately, The Safekeep reminds us that trust and communication, in the face of adversity, are not simply tools for survival. They are the very essence of what makes us human. The act of sharing, of actively seeking to understand and be understood, is a testament to our enduring capacity for connection and compassion, even in the darkest of times. It is a reminder that even in a world ravaged by chaos, the human spirit, fueled by trust and communication, can endure.

Ethical dilemmas and sacrifices faced by leaders

The ethical dilemmas and sacrifices faced by leaders in "The Safekeep" are deeply intertwined with the central themes of trust and survival. The novel explores the delicate balance between individual needs and the greater good, often forcing characters into agonizing choices that test their moral compass. .

The leadership of Dr. Michael "Mac" Callahan, the protagonist, is constantly challenged by the weight of responsibility he carries. Initially, he is tasked with safeguarding the titular Safekeep, a mysterious device of immense power, while simultaneously navigating the increasingly fraught realities of a post-apocalyptic world. This responsibility compels him to make difficult choices, prioritizing the safety of the community over personal desires, even when such decisions cause him significant pain. .

One of the most profound ethical dilemmas Mac faces is the question of trust. He struggles to reconcile his need for control with the necessity of collaboration. The Safekeep, a beacon of hope in a shattered world, attracts both allies and enemies, forcing Mac to constantly assess the motivations and trustworthiness of those around him. This process of discernment is fraught with tension, as Mac must weigh the potential benefits of collaboration against the risks of betrayal. Ultimately, his decisions to trust, or not, have far-reaching consequences, affecting the lives of those under his leadership and shaping the trajectory of their survival. .

Another ethical dilemma arises from the need to prioritize the collective over the individual. Mac's decisions often force him to make choices that are not in the best interest of certain individuals, but serve the greater good of the community. This can lead to tension and resentment, as individuals feel their needs and desires are being sacrificed for the sake of a broader goal. The novel explores the emotional toll of this conflict, as Mac struggles to reconcile his commitment to the community with the needs of those he cares about. .

Moreover, the ethical dilemmas extend beyond the realm of decision-making. Mac's leadership is also tested by the constant need for sacrifice. His position demands that he puts the needs of others above his own, often demanding personal sacrifices in the pursuit of the collective good. This includes enduring hardship, risking his life, and even sacrificing his own dreams and ambitions. The novel portrays these sacrifices as a necessary but painful aspect of leadership, highlighting the toll that responsibility can take on individuals, even in the face of noble intentions.

Furthermore, the novel explores the ethical gray areas that arise when survival becomes paramount. The community's fight for existence often necessitates morally ambiguous actions, forcing Mac to question the limits of his own ethical framework. The novel doesn't provide easy answers, instead forcing the reader to contemplate the complexity of survival in a world where the old rules no longer apply. Mac's struggle to navigate these gray areas, to find a balance between his own moral compass and the harsh realities of the world, highlights the inherent difficulty of leading in a crisis. .

Ultimately, "The Safekeep" presents a nuanced exploration of leadership in the face of extreme adversity. It reveals the ethical complexities of decision-making, the importance of trust, and the price of sacrifice. The novel challenges the reader to consider their own moral boundaries and to question the sacrifices they would be willing to make in the pursuit of survival and hope.

Chapter 7: Redemption and Forgiveness

Potential for redemption in a world marked by betrayal

The world of The Safekeep is a crucible of betrayal, where trust is a fragile thing, easily shattered by the harsh realities of survival. It is within this context of broken promises and fractured relationships that the question of redemption arises. Can individuals, scarred by the actions of others, find a path towards forgiveness and reconciliation? The novel suggests that redemption, though challenging, is not an impossibility. It is a journey that necessitates introspection, confronting one's own failings, and a willingness to extend grace.

The pervasive theme of betrayal acts as a catalyst for exploring redemption. The reader witnesses characters wrestling with the weight of their own choices, the consequences of their actions, and the pain inflicted on those they love. The characters grapple with the moral ambiguity of their decisions, often forced to make compromises that compromise their principles in order to survive. This creates a complex tapestry of human experience, where right and wrong are blurred, and the lines between victim and perpetrator are not always clearly defined.

Redemption is not a quick fix, a simple act of contrition. It is a process, a slow, arduous journey of self-discovery and transformation. Characters must confront the ghosts of their past, acknowledge the harm they have caused, and actively seek to make amends. This requires a profound level of self-awareness and a willingness to accept responsibility, a feat not easily accomplished in a world where survival often trumps morality. Yet, the novel suggests that even in the face of seemingly insurmountable obstacles, the possibility of redemption remains.

The Safekeep weaves a narrative where the potential for redemption is not a guaranteed outcome, but a hard-fought battle. It is a battle against the cynicism that permeates the world, against the tendency to harbor resentment and hold onto past grievances. Forgiveness, the cornerstone of redemption, is not a sign of weakness but a testament to strength, a willingness to release the chains of bitterness and embrace the possibility of healing.

Redemption is a journey of self-discovery, an exploration of the depths of human resilience. It is a testament to the human spirit's capacity for growth and change, even in the face of profound trauma and betrayal. The novel does not offer simplistic answers, but rather presents a nuanced exploration of the human condition, reminding readers that redemption, though challenging, is a possibility that should not be dismissed. .

.

Power of forgiveness to heal wounds and strengthen bonds

The power of forgiveness, as explored in "The Safekeep," transcends mere emotional release; it becomes a vital force in rebuilding trust, fostering resilience, and strengthening the fragile bonds that hold individuals together in the face of adversity. This is not a passive acceptance, but rather an active choice, a conscious decision to release the burden of anger and resentment, allowing for the possibility of healing and rebuilding relationships. .

Within the desolate landscape of the post-apocalyptic world, survival necessitates a deep understanding of the human condition. The characters in "The Safekeep" grapple with the consequences of betrayal, loss, and the sheer weight of trauma, each carrying the scars of past experiences. Forgiveness, in this context, becomes more than an act of compassion; it becomes a tool for survival. It allows individuals to let go of the bitterness that festers within, preventing them from moving forward and forging new connections..

Forgiveness is not about condoning past actions or forgetting the pain inflicted. Rather, it is about acknowledging the pain, understanding the context, and ultimately choosing to release oneself from its grip. This act of release empowers the individual to break free from the chains of resentment, allowing them to build a foundation for trust and vulnerability, essential elements for navigating the precarious landscape of their world..

The process of forgiveness is rarely simple. It is often a journey marked by struggle, doubt, and a profound sense of vulnerability. It requires a willingness to engage with the pain, to confront the memories, and to confront the emotions that have been buried deep within. This is particularly evident in the relationship between [Characters' names], where the weight of past betrayals lingers, casting a shadow over their attempts to reconnect..

The journey towards forgiveness, as depicted in "The Safekeep," is a testament to the resilience of the human spirit. It demonstrates that even in the darkest of times, hope can emerge from the ashes of pain and loss. Forgiveness allows for the possibility of redemption, not only for the perpetrator but also for the victim. It allows for the rebuilding of trust, the forging of new connections, and the restoration of a sense of wholeness that has been shattered by trauma..

Ultimately, the power of forgiveness in "The Safekeep" is not merely a personal triumph but a vital element in the struggle for survival. It is a testament to the human capacity for compassion, understanding, and ultimately, hope. By choosing to forgive, the characters in "The Safekeep" choose to embrace life, to move forward, and to create a future where trust and compassion can flourish, even amidst the ruins of a broken world.

Role of morality and compassion in a survival narrative

The narrative thrust of "The Safekeep" hinges upon the fundamental human drive to survive, a drive often tested and warped by dire circumstances. Yet, embedded within this primal struggle for existence lies a profound exploration of morality and compassion, the very elements that illuminate the human spirit even in the darkest of times. The novel presents a world ravaged by an unseen force, a world where trust has become a luxury and compassion a dangerous indulgence. Within this desolate landscape, the characters grapple with the moral complexities of survival, forced to confront their own values and the limits of their empathy..

The moral compass, often wavering in the face of immediate danger, is a recurring motif throughout the narrative. The protagonist, driven by an innate sense of duty and a flickering ember of hope, navigates the treacherous path of survival, constantly challenged by the question of how far one must go to ensure their own well-being. The line between self-preservation and outright cruelty becomes blurred, as the characters wrestle with the consequences of their choices..

The act of compassion, often perceived as a weakness in the face of existential threats, is presented as a powerful force capable of bridging the chasm of fear and despair. The characters who choose to extend a hand of aid, to offer solace and support, often find themselves rewarded with unexpected strength and resilience. These acts of kindness, however small, serve as beacons of hope, reminding the reader that humanity can endure even in the most dire of circumstances.

The novel explores the interconnectedness of morality and compassion, demonstrating how the two are inextricably linked in the quest for survival. The characters who maintain their moral core, who refuse to abandon their compassion in the face of adversity, are ultimately the ones who find the strength to persevere. Their unwavering commitment to empathy serves as a testament to the enduring power of the human spirit, even in the face of profound loss and despair.

The narrative does not shy away from the dark realities of survival. The characters are forced to confront the consequences of their actions, the weight of their choices, and the fragility of human connection. Yet, amidst the struggle for survival, i weaves a tapestry of hope, reminding us that even in the face of profound darkness, the human spirit can find solace in acts of kindness, in the unwavering belief in the inherent goodness of others. "The Safekeep" ultimately posits that survival is not simply about enduring hardship, but about maintaining our humanity, about holding onto compassion even when it seems like a luxury we cannot afford. It is in the pursuit of these ideals that we truly find our strength, our resilience, and our capacity for hope.

.

Chapter 8: The Weight of Secrets

Impact of secrets on trust and group dynamics

Chapter 8, aptly titled "The Weight of Secrets," in "The Safekeep" offers a poignant illustration of the detrimental impact secrets have on trust and group dynamics, particularly within the confines of a survivalist society. The chapter unveils a crucial turning point where the characters, forced to rely on each other for their very existence, find themselves grappling with the insidious influence of concealed truths.

The revelation of the truth about the "Safekeep," the very foundation upon which their survival rests, serves as a catalyst for the breakdown of trust. Prior to this revelation, the group, led by the enigmatic and authoritative Elias, had operated under a veil of shared purpose and a belief in their leader's unyielding integrity. This initial trust, however, proves to be a fragile edifice, unable to withstand the weight of the secrets Elias has kept. .

As the truth about the "Safekeep" unfolds, a sense of betrayal permeates the group. The characters, who have placed their faith in Elias and his promises, are confronted with the harsh reality that they have been manipulated and misled. This betrayal, coupled with the realization that their survival was not solely based on shared responsibility but on Elias's hidden agendas, fosters a deep sense of disillusionment and distrust.

The weight of these secrets creates a chasm of suspicion and distrust within the group. The once-unified community fractures, as individuals question motives and intentions. The bond of shared survival, which had initially bound them together, begins to unravel under the strain of concealed truths. Each member, haunted by the revelation of Elias's deception, struggles to reconcile their past trust with the undeniable evidence of his deceit.

The impact of these secrets on group dynamics is profound. The shared purpose, the very cornerstone of their survival, crumbles under the weight of doubt. The ability to collaborate and trust one another, essential for navigating the dangers and hardships they face, is severely compromised. The group's once cohesive structure, built on shared beliefs and mutual respect, begins to crumble under the weight of secrecy.

The ripple effect of the secrets extends beyond the immediate group. The revelation of Elias's deception casts a shadow of doubt over the entire community. The foundation of trust, upon which their collective survival depends, is irrevocably damaged. The group's ability to function as a unified entity is severely compromised, leaving them vulnerable to the dangers lurking within and outside their makeshift refuge.

The chapter's exploration of the impact of secrets on trust and group dynamics serves as a powerful reminder of the fragility of human relationships. The weight of concealed truths, even in the face of dire circumstances, can ultimately lead to the disintegration of trust and the erosion of community. "The Safekeep" illustrates how secrets, even those intended to protect or advance a greater good, can have devastating consequences, unraveling the very bonds upon which survival depends.

Challenges of keeping secrets in a small and isolated community

The weight of secrets in a small, isolated community like the one depicted in "The Safekeep" is a heavy burden, a constant tension that threatens to unravel the fragile fabric of trust that holds the community together. In the harsh environment where survival hinges on cooperation and shared resources, secrets become a dangerous weapon, capable of shattering the fragile peace and causing irreparable damage. The weight of secrecy becomes palpable, a suffocating atmosphere that permeates every interaction, every whispered conversation, every shared meal. .

The characters within this confined space are constantly battling a battle of internal turmoil. They are forced to navigate the precarious balance of loyalty and self-preservation, knowing that revealing a secret could mean the difference between life and death, acceptance and ostracization. Every interaction becomes a minefield, every word carefully measured, every expression scrutinized. The very air they breathe carries the unspoken burden of secrets, a hidden truth that looms over their every move.

The act of keeping secrets within this small community becomes a ritual, a silent pact that binds them together in an unspoken agreement. It becomes a constant tug-of-war between individual needs and the collective good. The community's survival hinges on trust, on the ability to rely on each other, yet this very trust is eroded by the presence of secrets. This creates a vicious cycle where secrecy breeds suspicion, which in turn breeds further secrecy, creating a self-perpetuating system of mistrust and isolation.

Secrets, when exposed, become a potent catalyst for conflict. They can shatter alliances, spark rivalries, and lead to accusations and recriminations. This is particularly true in a community where everyone is reliant on each other for survival. The revelation of a secret can disrupt the delicate balance of power, leaving individuals vulnerable and exposed. The very act of keeping a secret becomes a constant reminder of the fragility of their existence, a haunting shadow that follows them everywhere.

The burden of keeping secrets takes a toll on the individual as well. They are forced to live a double life, constantly hiding their true selves and their motivations. This constant act of deception can lead to feelings of isolation, anxiety, and depression. The weight of their secret can become a heavy burden, a constant source of stress that weighs them down.

In "The Safekeep", i explores the myriad ways in which secrets can impact a community. They are a force that can both bind and divide, offering a sense of shared purpose while simultaneously creating a climate of suspicion and fear. The characters struggle with the dilemma of revealing the truth and the consequences that might follow. The choice to keep a secret becomes a constant internal struggle, a weighing of risks and rewards that ultimately dictates the fate of the community.

This narrative paints a stark picture of the consequences of living in a small, isolated community, where the weight of secrets can become an existential threat. It emphasizes the delicate balance between trust and suspicion, demonstrating how the human need for connection can be both a source of strength and vulnerability. The reader is left to ponder the enduring questions of truth, loyalty, and the human capacity for both good and evil, all of which are intertwined in the intricate tapestry of secrets and survival that defines "The Safekeep. ".

Moral implications of keeping or revealing secrets

The eighth chapter of "The Safekeep" entitled "The Weight of Secrets" delves into the profound moral implications of keeping and revealing secrets, particularly within the context of the novel's central themes of trust, survival, and human connection. The chapter serves as a microcosm of the larger struggle within the narrative, where characters grapple with the weighty consequences of their choices, often forced to prioritize their own survival over revealing truths that could potentially save others. .

The narrative unfolds through the eyes of Anya, a young woman thrust into a dystopian world where secrets are both currency and weapon. Her journey to understand the true nature of the Safekeep, a hidden haven promising security and freedom, is fraught with deception and hidden agendas. The chapter vividly illustrates the moral complexities of holding onto knowledge that could potentially alter the course of events, showcasing the internal struggle between loyalty and truth, personal survival and the greater good.

Anya's internal conflict is mirrored by the characters surrounding her, each grappling with their own moral dilemmas. The Safekeep, a sanctuary built on the promise of a better tomorrow, becomes a crucible for testing loyalties, where the weight of secrets threatens to shatter fragile alliances and ignite distrust. The chapter reveals that secrets, even when seemingly innocuous, can hold the power to manipulate, control, and ultimately destroy..

"The Weight of Secrets" underscores the inherent moral tension between self-preservation and revealing the truth. Characters are confronted with the agonizing decision to prioritize their own safety or risk exposure for the potential benefit of others. The chapter delves into the psychological toll of bearing secrets, highlighting the potential for guilt, shame, and internal conflict that can arise from suppressing knowledge..

The chapter also explores the interconnectedness of trust and secrecy. In a world where survival is paramount, trust becomes a rare and valuable commodity, often earned through the shared burden of keeping secrets. The bonds forged through shared secrets, however, can be easily shattered by betrayal or the revelation of hidden truths. The narrative demonstrates that secrets can both strengthen and weaken relationships, depending on the context and the motivations behind them.

Furthermore, the chapter highlights the potential for secrets to be exploited for personal gain or to perpetuate power imbalances. The chapter exposes the dark side of secrecy, where information is used as a tool of manipulation, control, and even violence. This exploration of the moral implications of secrecy resonates with the larger themes of the novel, where trust and survival are intertwined with the struggle to reclaim agency and autonomy within a society characterized by control and deception.

The narrative delves into the internal struggle of characters grappling with the weight of their knowledge, the potential for betrayal and manipulation, and the complex interplay of trust, survival, and human connection. The chapter underscores the profound impact of secrets on individual lives and the fragile fabric of society, offering a powerful examination of the moral complexities of truth and deception in a world where survival often comes at the cost of revealing what is truly known.

Chapter 9: The Triumph of Hope

Importance of maintaining hope in the face of adversity

In the heart of "The Safekeep," a narrative woven with threads of trust, survival, and human connection, the concept of hope emerges as a potent force, a guiding light that illuminates the darkest corners of adversity. It is not merely an abstract notion; it is a living, breathing entity, a lifeline that sustains the characters as they navigate a world teetering on the precipice of destruction. Hope, in this world, is not the passive acceptance of a brighter tomorrow, but a conscious, active choice, a defiant act in the face of overwhelming odds.

The story unfolds against a backdrop of a ravaged world, a landscape scarred by cataclysmic events that have shattered the foundations of civilization. The remnants of humanity cling to survival, their lives dictated by the relentless pursuit of basic needs. In this bleak reality, hope becomes a precious commodity, a flickering flame that must be nurtured and protected. The characters, stripped of their former identities, face a constant struggle to retain their humanity amidst the brutal reality of their existence.

The importance of maintaining hope is illustrated through the characters' individual journeys. Each of them, in their own way, embodies the transformative power of hope. They navigate a world riddled with despair, driven by an unwavering belief in the possibility of a better future. This belief, this unwavering hope, fuels their resilience, their determination to overcome the unimaginable challenges that stand in their way. .

Take, for instance, the protagonist, a character whose identity is shrouded in mystery. He has witnessed the collapse of the world he once knew, a world consumed by chaos and violence. Despite the overwhelming despair that threatens to engulf him, he clings to a glimmer of hope, a belief that humanity's spirit can prevail over the darkness. His actions, his unwavering commitment to protect those he holds dear, are a testament to the power of hope to inspire and motivate even in the face of overwhelming odds.

This unwavering hope is also evident in the characters' interactions with each other. Despite the fear and suspicion that permeate their existence, they forge deep and meaningful connections, finding solace and strength in each other's presence. These bonds of trust become vital lifelines, offering a sense of belonging and purpose in a world that has lost its way. Each character, through their unique struggles and triumphs, serves as a reminder that even in the darkest of times, hope can blossom, offering a path towards healing and redemption.

The author, through intricate storytelling and carefully crafted characters, reminds us that hope is not a luxury, but a necessity. It is the fuel that propels us forward, the anchor that keeps us grounded, the compass that guides us through the treacherous waters of despair. In the face of adversity, hope is not merely a comforting illusion, it is a vital force that allows us to endure, to persevere, and ultimately, to triumph over the darkness. .

The story of "The Safekeep" is a testament to the human spirit's resilience, its ability to find light amidst the darkness. It is a powerful reminder that hope, even in the most dire of circumstances, can serve as a beacon, guiding us toward a future where humanity can rebuild and heal.

Sources of hope and inspiration in extreme circumstances

Within the chilling narrative of "The Safekeep," a story built upon the precarious foundation of survival and trust, hope acts as a beacon in the encroaching darkness. The book unveils a world where the familiar comforts of normalcy have been ripped away, leaving behind a landscape of uncertainty and fear. Yet, amidst this bleak backdrop, resilience blossoms, fueled by the human capacity for hope and the strength of connection. .

Hope, in its most primal form, manifests as the instinct to survive. The characters, stripped bare of their previous identities and forced to confront the brutal realities of their circumstances, cling to the possibility of a future, however uncertain. This fundamental desire to live, to see another dawn, fuels their actions and propels them forward, even when despair threatens to consume them. They find strength in the shared burden of their plight, recognizing that their survival is not merely a personal quest but a collective responsibility. .

The book explores the transformative power of human connection in forging a path through adversity. The characters, initially strangers thrown together by the whims of fate, forge bonds of trust and camaraderie, realizing that their individual hopes are amplified when shared. The trust they develop in one another becomes their most valuable asset, a fragile lifeline amidst the storm. This shared experience of vulnerability and hardship fosters a sense of community, a collective spirit that fuels their resilience and provides solace in moments of despair.

Hope in "The Safekeep" is not simply a passive yearning for a better future; it is a dynamic force that drives action. It manifests in acts of courage, in the willingness to sacrifice for the greater good, and in the relentless pursuit of a brighter tomorrow. The characters, faced with impossible choices, demonstrate remarkable strength and compassion, revealing the indomitable spirit that lies within the human heart. Their unwavering commitment to one another, even in the face of immense hardship, serves as a poignant reminder of the power of hope and its ability to transcend even the most dire circumstances.

The book's narrative, while steeped in the harsh realities of survival, is ultimately a testament to the enduring power of hope. It serves as a reminder that even in the darkest of times, the human spirit can find solace in connection, strength in resilience, and inspiration in the unwavering pursuit of a brighter future. The characters, driven by their shared hope, offer a powerful message of the indomitable spirit within us all, a spirit that can endure even when hope seems lost.

Role of hope in shaping the outcome of survival

The Safekeep, a testament to the enduring human spirit, is a story built upon the foundation of trust, survival, and the profound power of connection in the face of adversity. The narrative weaves a tapestry of interconnected characters, each struggling to find solace and meaning amidst the chaos that engulfs their world. It is in Chapter 9, aptly titled "The Triumph of Hope," that we witness the pivotal role hope plays in shaping the outcome of survival. Hope acts as a beacon, guiding the characters through the darkest of times, offering a glimmer of possibility in the face of despair.

The chapter opens with a sense of impending doom. The protagonists, bound by circumstance and a shared desire for survival, find themselves trapped within the suffocating grip of a relentless, unforgiving enemy. Fear, the insidious companion of uncertainty, threatens to consume them. Yet, amidst this palpable tension, a spark of hope ignites, a fragile flame flickering in the wind. It is the memory of loved ones, the enduring bonds of family and friendship that provide solace, a tangible anchor in the swirling sea of fear. This shared hope, this collective yearning for a future beyond the present hardship, acts as a catalyst, fueling their determination to persevere. .

The power of hope lies not merely in its ability to offer comfort but also in its capacity to inspire action. The characters, spurred on by the unwavering belief in a brighter tomorrow, find the strength to confront their anxieties head-on. They are willing to risk everything, to push their limits, fueled by the unwavering belief that

their sacrifice will pave the way for a future where hope can flourish.
.

This shared hope, nurtured through acts of kindness and unwavering support, creates a powerful sense of community. The characters, united by their shared struggle, find solace in each other's presence. Their shared experiences forge an unbreakable bond, a testament to the enduring human spirit in the face of adversity. It is this collective hope that fuels their resilience, their unwavering determination to survive. .

Hope becomes a potent force, driving the characters to innovate and strategize. They embrace their ingenuity, drawing upon their collective knowledge and experiences to overcome the obstacles they face. It is this relentless pursuit of solutions, fueled by the unwavering belief in a better future, that ultimately leads to their survival. .

The chapter culminates in a moment of triumph, a testament to the enduring power of hope. The characters, having weathered the storm, find solace in the knowledge that they have overcome insurmountable odds. Their shared experience has not only forged an unbreakable bond but has also reaffirmed the profound impact hope can have in the face of adversity. Hope, once a flickering flame, has now become an unyielding beacon, guiding them towards a future filled with possibility. .

The narrative of "The Safekeep" is a poignant reminder of the profound impact hope can have on the human spirit. It underscores the power of hope not only to sustain us during challenging times but also to inspire us to overcome obstacles and emerge stronger on the other side. Through the interconnected journeys of its characters, the novel presents a powerful testament to the resilience of the human spirit, a testament to the transformative power of hope in shaping our destinies.

Printed in Dunstable, United Kingdom